Maggie
and the Emergency Room

written by
Martine Davison

illustrated by
Marylin Hafner

Random House New York

Text copyright © 1992 by American Medical Association and Random House, Inc. Illustrations copyright © 1992 by Marylin Hafner. All rights reserved under International and Pan-American Copyright Conventions. Published in the United States by Random House, Inc., New York, and simultaneously in Canada by Random House of Canada Limited, Toronto.
Library of Congress Cataloging-in-Publication Data
Davison, Martine. A visit to the emergency room / by Martine Davison : illustrated by Marylin Hafner.   p.   cm. — (An AMA kids book)
   Summary: When Maggie falls off her bike, her mother takes her to be examined, x-rayed, and stitched in the emergency room of a nearby hospital.   ISBN 0-679-81818-9 — ISBN 0-679-91818-3 (lib. bdg.)   [1. Hospitals—Emergency service—Fiction.   2. Medical care—Fiction.]   I. Hafner, Marylin, Ill.   II. Title.   III. Series.
PZ7.D3215Vi   1992 [E]—dc20   91-31413   Manufactured in the United States of America   10 9 8 7 6 5 4 3 2 1

Bump. Bump. Bump went the wheels of their bikes. It wasn't a very good place to ride, down a winding dirt path through the woods of Hillsdale Park. But it was an adventure. *Bump. Bump. Bump.* First came Rita, then came Robby, and last of all, on her training wheels, came Maggie.

Suddenly, Rita called, "Watch out!"
Robby swerved just in time, but Maggie went bumpety-bump over a big fat tree root. Over her handlebars she flew.

The next thing she knew, Maggie was lying on the ground.
Rita and Robby were standing over her.
"You're bleeding!" Rita cried.

Robby rode like the wind to get Mrs. Barton, Maggie's mother.

Ten minutes later Maggie was in the front seat of her mother's station wagon, holding her favorite stuffed animal, Binkie, on her lap while her mother drove carefully but quickly to the emergency room of Hillsdale Memorial Hospital.

The admitting area of the emergency room was a busy place! In the middle of all the hustle and bustle a nurse sat calmly. Maggie spelled out the sign on the front of her desk. "T-R-I-A-G-E."

"It's pronounced *tree-ahj*," said Mrs. Barton. "It's a system of sorting people out into three groups: people hurt so badly they must be seen right away; people who can wait a little while; and people who can be seen after the other two groups have already been taken care of."

"I'll be with you in a second," the triage nurse told them. "Have a seat."

Maggie and her mother sat down on some chairs that just happened to be Maggie's favorite color. The floor was shiny, and the lights were very bright. Maggie looked around.

She saw an older woman sitting with her eyes closed, breathing noisily. She saw a teenage boy with his ankle wrapped in a towel. She saw a man with a brand-new cast on his arm.

A woman holding a baby was trying to talk to the triage nurse over her baby's crying. The nurse put something in the baby's ear.

"What's the nurse doing?" Maggie wanted to know.

"She's using a special new thermometer," Mrs. Barton explained, "that takes your temperature in no time at all."

"I hope the baby's all right," said Maggie. The baby wasn't much younger than Maggie's brother, Jerome. Mrs. Barton had left Jerome with the next-door neighbor.

"Maggie Barton!" called the triage nurse.

"That's us," said Mrs. Barton.

The triage nurse smiled and pointed to a woman sitting at a nearby desk. "That lady needs to ask you a few questions first."

The woman asked Maggie her name, her birth date, and whether she had any allergies. She typed the answers as Maggie gave them. Then she asked Maggie's mom even more questions. When was the last time Maggie had gotten a tetanus shot? How did they plan to pay? Maggie's mom handed the woman her insurance card. The woman typed some more, then pushed a button and walked over to a table. A machine wound out a sheet of paper and a strip of plastic.

The woman tore off the paper and fastened it to a clipboard. "This is your chart," she explained to Maggie.

Then she tore off the strip of plastic. She fastened it around Maggie's wrist. "And this is your ID bracelet."

Then the woman sent Maggie and her mom back to the triage desk.

"What happened to you?" the triage nurse wanted to know. Maggie told her all about riding her bike on the dirt path. It made Maggie feel special that the nurse wrote down everything she said.

The nurse took Maggie's blood pressure and her pulse. And she even put one of those new thermometers in Maggie's ear. It tickled!

The nurse asked, "Do you feel dizzy?"
"No," Maggie answered.
"Do you feel sick to your stomach?"
"You mean like I need to throw up? Nope."
The nurse smiled. "Does your head hurt?"
"A teeny tiny bit," said Maggie. "But not too bad."
The nurse put a bandage on Maggie's head.

Maggie and her mom followed the nurse through some sliding doors to an area where there were lots of small rooms. Maggie got to ride in a wheelchair.

Outside, Maggie heard the wail of a siren. Above the doors, at the end of a long hall, a red light started blinking. Seconds later four people burst through the doors wheeling a woman on a stretcher. A man ran in front of them and cleared a path into one of the small rooms. He shoved aside the curtains. More people ran into the room, wheeling equipment and talking quickly to one another.

"People sure move fast here," said Maggie a little uneasily.

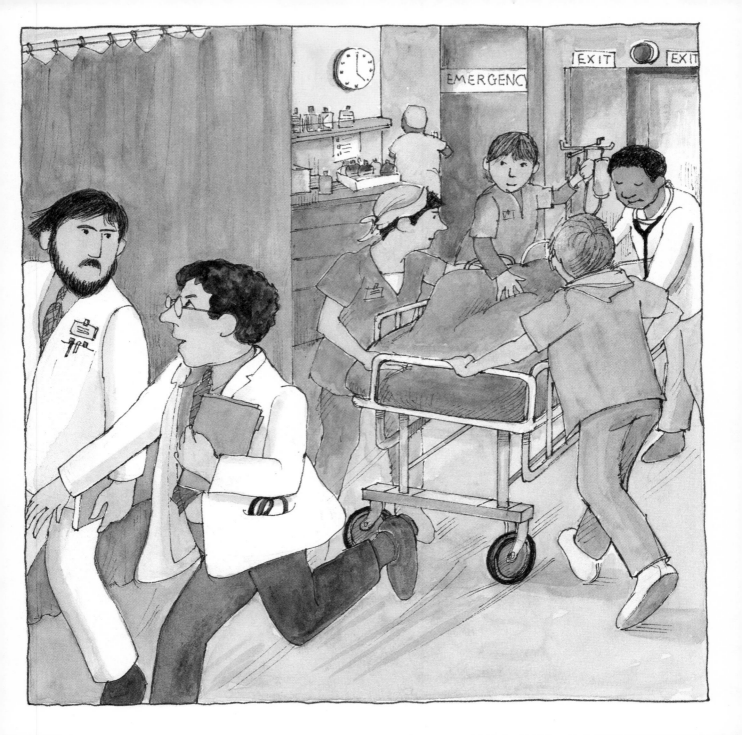

The nurse wheeled Maggie down the hall to the radiology room.

A woman named Bonnie spread a heavy blanket over Maggie. Binkie was cozy underneath it. The camera was gigantic. Mrs. Barton went to stand in a little room and watch through a window. Maggie felt a little scared.

"Why can't my mommy stay with me?" she asked Bonnie.

"Because the rays are very powerful. Powerful enough to look inside your body. You should only get them when you absolutely need them. So your mom and I will stand behind the glass. You'll be okay and you won't feel anything. Just hold very still and it won't take very long."

Maggie held very still. Bonnie left to go stand behind the glass with Mrs. Barton. The camera made a clicking noise. Bonnie came back out.

"Is the camera broken?" Maggie asked worriedly.

Bonnie laughed. "Oh no! That's the noise it makes when it's working. You've been the best patient I've had all day. And you've been very brave."

YOU'VE BEEN MY **BEST** PATIENT!

Next, the nurse wheeled Maggie into another room. "This is nice!" she exclaimed. "Not what I thought a hospital would be like."

In a few minutes another nurse came in. This nurse was a man. He looked at Maggie's cut very carefully. He left, saying, "Hang on. The doctor will be with you soon."

Maggie stared at the posters and waited. And waited. And waited. Was the doctor ever going to come?

Finally, the door opened.

"Hello, Mrs. Barton. Hello, Maggie. I'm Dr. Segundo."

Like everyone else here, the doctor seemed nice but very busy. She got right down to business. "Do you have a headache, Maggie?" she asked.

"A teeny tiny one. But I don't feel dizzy, and I don't feel like I need to throw up, either."

The doctor smiled. "You're way ahead of me, Maggie." The doctor took out a small flashlight and shined it into Maggie's eyes, then turned it off. Then she stood back. "How many fingers am I holding up, Maggie?"

"Easy!" Maggie said. "Four."

"That fall didn't hurt your eyes, did it?" said the doctor.

Dr. Segundo looked at the cut carefully and then cleaned it. It stung! Maggie squeezed Binkie with one hand and her mother's hand with the other.

"You're a lucky girl," said the doctor. "It's not a very deep cut. But I'm going to give you a couple of stitches so that when it's healed you won't have a big scar."

"Okay," Maggie said slowly, but she was a little scared.

The doctor sprayed Maggie's forehead with something that felt cold and tingly. In a second her forehead was numb, as if she had held an ice cube to it. Then the doctor injected a medicine that stung for just a second. Maggie's mom held her hand.

"Don't move, Maggie," said the doctor.

Maggie held herself statue-still while the doctor did the most amazing thing! She sewed Maggie's head—with a needle and thread.

"Just like I sewed Binkie once!" Maggie breathed.

"Really?" said the doctor. "Did Binkie fall off her bike too?"

"Oh no! My baby brother, Jerome, chewed him."

The doctor stood back. "All done!"

"Already?" Maggie asked. "That wasn't *too* bad."

"In five days you can go to your own doctor to have the stitches removed."

The doctor put a bandage over the cut.
"Thanks! Now can I go home?" asked Maggie.
"Just as soon as you promise you'll wear a helmet when you ride a bicycle, just like racing-car drivers do," said the doctor.

In the parking lot Maggie said, "Wait till I tell Rita and Robby about my trip to the emergency room."

"I hope that's the last time you take a trip down that dirt trail on your bicycle, young lady," said Maggie's mother. "Accidents do happen, but you need to be more careful so they don't happen in the first place."

TO PARKING

"From now on we'll stick to the bike paths," Maggie promised. Just then she saw the woman with the baby who had been inside. The baby wasn't crying anymore. Maggie held up Binkie and made her wave bye-bye to the baby. The baby held up a chubby fist and waved bye-bye back. Then she broke into a big toothless grin.

"It looks like I'm not the only one who's glad to be going home!" Maggie said as she and Binkie got into the front seat and buckled their seat belts.